Ollie's Class Trip

A YES-and-NO Book

by Stephanie Calmenson

illustrated by Abby Carter

Holiday House / New York

To Noah and Justin —S. C.

To Bob and Julie —A. C.

Text copyright © 2015 by Stephanie Calmenson
Illustrations copyright © 2015 by Abby Carter
All Rights Reserved
HOLIDAY HOUSE is registered in the U.S. Patent and Trademark Office.
Printed and Bound in April 2015 at Toppan Leefung, DongGuan City, China.
The artwork was created with watercolors.
www.holidayhouse.com
First Edition
1 3 5 7 9 10 8 6 4 2

Library of Congress Cataloging-in-Publication Data
Calmenson, Stephanie.
Ollie's class trip : a yes-and-no book / by Stephanie Calmenson ; illustrated by Abby Carter. — First edition.
pages cm
Summary: Asks the reader a series of yes or no questions as Ollie and his classmates visit an aquarium.
ISBN 978-0-8234-3432-9 (hardcover)
[1. School field trips—Fiction. 2. Aquariums—Fiction. 3. Questions and answers.] I. Carter, Abby, illustrator. II. Title.
PZ7.C1360j 2015
[E]—dc23
2014044162

Do you want to hear an Ollie story?

YES!

Good! Let's get started.

"Good morning, class," says Ollie's teacher.
"Today is our class trip."

Where will Ollie's class go?

To the moon?

NO!

Up into a
bluebird's nest?

NO!

Sliding down a rainbow?

NO!

Will Ollie's class go to the aquarium?

YES!

Who will be Ollie's trip buddy?

Will it be his cat, Binky?

NO!

Will it be a kangaroo?

NO!

Will it be Humpty Dumpty?

NO!

Will Ollie's trip buddy be his good friend Tate?

YES!

How will the class get to the aquarium?

Will they go in a submarine? NO!

Will they fly there like kites? NO!

Will they roll to the aquarium like bowling balls? NO!

Will Ollie's class ride the school bus?

YES!

What will Ollie see at the aquarium?

Will he see mooing cows?

NO!

Will he see kittens and puppies?

NO!

Will he see lions and tigers and bears?

NO!

Will Ollie see amazing animals that live in and around the water?

YES!

What will Ollie do when Mike,
the aquarium guide,
is talking to the class?

Will Ollie tell
jokes to a shark?

NO!

Will he take a ride on a sea horse?

NO!

Will he play tag with a turtle?

NO!

Will Ollie have fun
looking, listening
and learning?

Ollie's teacher tells the class that there's a special surprise for them at the aquarium.
"Please take your buddy's hand and follow me," she says.

Uh-oh! Ollie can't find Tate.
What will he do?

Will Ollie run away from the class
to look for his friend?

NO!

Will he sit down and cry
great big crocodile tears?

NO!

Will he call a jellyfish detective
and report his friend missing?

NO!

Will Ollie quickly tell his teacher
that he can't find Tate?

YES!

Ollie's happy to see Tate again.
Now Ollie can think about the special surprise.
What do you think the surprise might be?

A ride on an octobus?

NO!

A grape jellyfish sandwich?

NO!

An autograph from a
world-famous starfish?

NO!

Will the surprise be a baby beluga's birthday party?

YES!

What will the belugas
do at the party?

Will they play Pin the Tail
on the Whale?

NO!

Will they open presents?

NO!

Will they blow out candles on a cake?

NO!

Will they dive and leap and eat fish treats?

YES!

When it's time to go, Ollie and his friends
each get a birthday cupcake. Yum!
Ollie had a great time on his class trip.
Would you like to go on a class trip too?

YES!

Ollie's Class Trip "Yes" List

Will you always make sure you
can *see* a teacher or parent? YES!

YES!

Will you listen to your teacher and follow directions?

Will you hold your buddy's hand when walking? YES!

If you can't find your buddy,
will you tell your teacher
right away? YES!

If you ever get separated from
your class, will you stay where
you are and tell a grown-up?

YES!

Will you have fun
on your class trip?

YES!

I had fun,
Mommy!

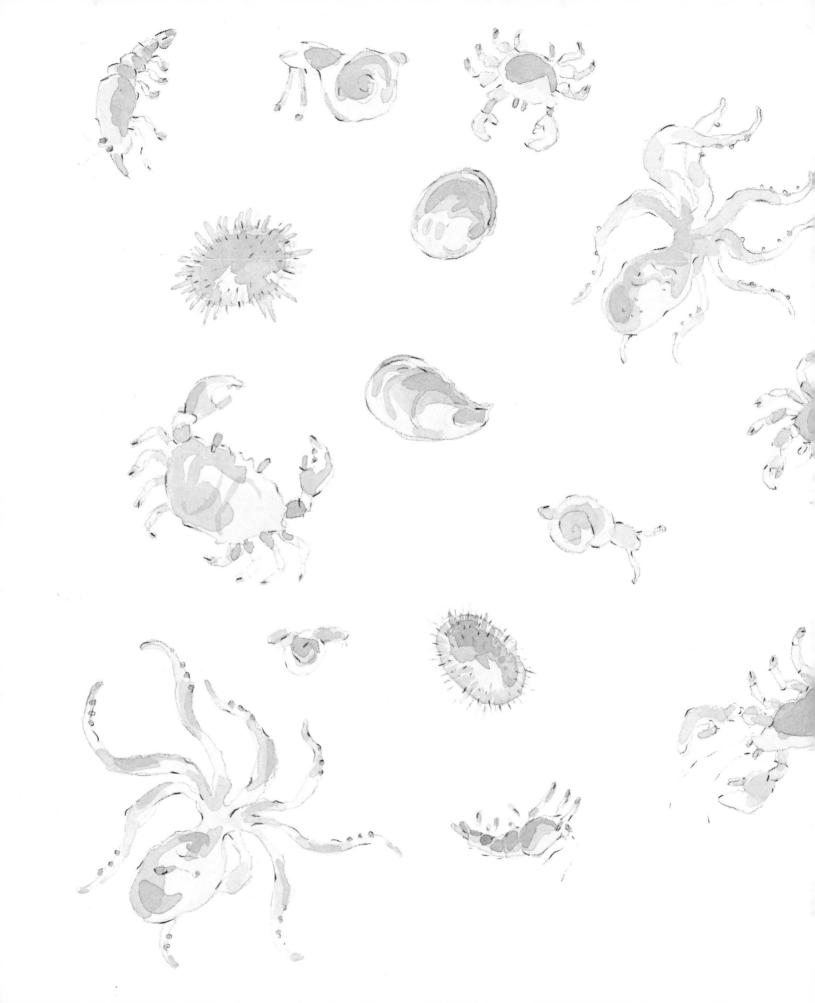